Unique - Short - Stories and Fables

March 23, 2024

To Miguela:
Be Colorful - My Great Friend
Thank you for your support.

Love Always and Forever

Lola J. Hobbs

— Enjoy! —

Unique - Short - Stories and Fables
By: Lola J. Hobbs

Disclaimer:

This is a work of fiction. Names, characters, places, and incidents are products of the author's imagination and are used fictitiously. Any resemblance to the actual person's living or dead or actual events is purely coincidental.

Copyright: By Lola J Hobbs 2024 ©

All rights reserved. No part of this publication may be reproduced, distributed, or transmitted in any form by any means, including photocopying, recording, or other electronic or mechanical methods, without the prior written permission from the author, except for viewers who quote brief passages in a review from my appreciated book readers.

PLEASE ENJOY THE BOOK WITH GREAT PHOTOS!

Thank you so so much for purchasing my book. A creative life is an amplified life - creativity is a chaotic process. I wrote this book from my heart and soul. I hope you enjoy the stories- they are all different - that's why I call them unique. A reflection of my quirky personality. Some of them are fairy tales, animal stories, some are a bit dark, and of course a few love stories. ENJOY!

There are quite a few goose stories- you see I discovered the Canada geese at the golf course at Heather Gardens, in April 2020, after my large company TERMINATED all of us through an email. I was outraged! It was a warm sunny day, being a new resident here I had not been to the golf course, so I took a walk there and discovered the Canada geese and their adorable goslings. I became fascinated with them and walked every day just to see them. I closely observed them, read books about the Canada geese, and researched online. I started speaking to others about them, anyone who would have a positive story. After three months of intense studies, I wrote my first book titled Feathers at Echo Lake Part 1.

I have never written a book before but have always intended to. I give all the credit to these marvelous creatures who transformed my life. They are my Zen! Later I wrote my next book Feathers at Echo Lake Part 2.

Believe me when I say this - I would have never written these books if I hadn't found these Canada geese and their families. I closely studied their behavior. I am amazed because these creatures are highly intelligent. In the spring you will see a few fights among the males [ganders]. They are protective of their mates, their territory, and their goslings.

I count and name them sometimes. Residents and golfers laugh at me, that's okay I don't mind. Trust me when I say this - there are NO resident geese here, at Heather Gardens. You will always see some geese at the golf course, and among other areas constantly because this is a stopover for the geese to rest and feed while traveling to their destination or back to their original home site. OUR geese always migrate. Migration is extremely difficult for them, many sadly don't survive.

If you live here, or just visiting, you will see me with my phone taking videos and photos of them regularly. Many people have named me Mother Goose, which I take as a compliment - thank you. Therefore, I am very passionate about them so please if you have ANY NEGATIVE comments about them PLEASE - Just Walk On By - you can call me crazy or whatever. It's quite possible, you don't have a clear understanding of them. The Canada geese are somewhat human-like.

The gander [daddy] is extremely protective when they have their goslings in the spring. The parents will hiss at people because they feel like their babies could be harmed. Because of this people feel like they are being aggressive well maybe they are a bit except PLEASE try to understand them - have a heart! Our geese are tamed except, they're on constant watch because there are plenty of the FOX and COYOTES that roam around even during the day at the golf course. THEY are predators and are anxious to feed their young, THEY are getting pretty daring. So please be careful because THEY will harm you!

You are also protective of your family and your pets are you not? EXACTLY! Sincerely, Lola J. Hobbs

DEDICATION

My dedication to this book is true to my Mom and Dad.

Who look at me sweetly from the Heavens above.

They gave me the courage to create a book I have always wanted to write.

DEDICATION CONTINUED

AMY IANNONE - MY SISTER AND MY BEST FRIEND

Who has been there through my highs and lows
I have had unfortunately way too many LOWS - Just like many people
Including Amy - but you would never know

She understands me more than anyone else
We are a different flower from the same garden - She feels my pain and joy
Amy is always there for me no matter what she is so busy with her business
Professional Bookkeeping and Tax Assistance Yet she always makes the time

Listens to everything I have to say and relates to everything more
than anyone on the planet. She was extremely excited that I finally started
writing books because I talked about it a lot and never did it.
I am so very proud of you and all of your accomplishments and everything that
you've been through you are my STRENGTH EVERYDAY!!!

Thank you for always being there for me - our mom passed away when you
were only 11 years old - your teenage years were quite a challenge for me!
Only - you laugh about them and tell me you were just preparing me for when I
have my children.

Something you're very good at is laughing at things that aren't funny
therefore you turn it around for me - I could not do this on my own.
When friends are not enough - I'm glad I have your phone number

You are such a fabulous mother, grandma and a great cook
Thank you for challenging me - Your positive energy gives me the flow to keep
on going - I feel it - even though you aren't here beside me. This must be
coming from your extremely positive energy.

Thank you for accepting me for being my eccentric self with my vivid imagination. Only you can follow my conversations that are all over the place with my severe ADHD!

Amy you are amazing! Our mom can see it - she smiles as she sips on her hot English tea in heaven

I love you so very much - thank you for always being - the best sister ever! I don't know what I'd do without you!

ADMIRATION - ERIC McCORMACK

Born in Toronto Canada, April 18th 1963 - I definitely have a thing for Canadians. Hence, my favorite wildlife is the Canada geese.

Eric started his career as an actor working many plays throughout Canada and for five seasons with the Stratford Shakespeare Festival.

He made his first Broadway starring as The Music Man. In 2012 he starred opposite James Earl Jones, Candice Bergen, and Angelina Lansbury in The Broadway Revival, The Best Man.

The following year he produced and starred in the role of Senator Cantrell in the same production. He also wrote the lyrics and sang " Living with Grace" music written by Barry Manilow, found on YouTube. Please check this out! Recorded the song The Greatest Discovery written by Elton John and Bernie Taupin.

Eric is best known as his main character part as Will in Will & Grace the comedy series that ran eight seasons starting in 1998-2006 and then ran three more seasons starting in 2017. He was a straight man playing a gay man. Remarkable and unbelievably funny! Bravo to those incredible writers and the entire cast. With cameos from many famous artists. I just finished enjoying the series {In which I watched them four times} for this Eric won the Emmy in 2001 for Best Outstanding Lead Actor in a Comedy Series.

I also loved the Hallmark movie Borrowed Hearts- I watched this a few times as I could not get enough of his smile! Also the voice of Garth in Guiding Emily. He was excellent in the crime drama series Perception. Except I wanted more seasons! I believe all of his work is exceptional, but most of all my admiration goes to him for his deep awareness and dedication to:

ADMIRATION CONTINUED - ERIC McCORMACK

ASPCA 2021 Compassion Award for his long-standing support of the ASPCA mission. " His compassionate commitment has inspired countless friends and fans to step out and speak out for animals in need." quote from Matt Bershadker, ASPCA President and CEO.

Other organizations include Project Angel Food, the official celebrity spokesman for the Canadian Cancer Society, Alzheimer's Association, Dream Foundation, Elton John's AIDS Foundation, Artists For Peace and City of Hope.

He is a profound supporter of the LGBTQ community and was given the Impact Award at the Point Foundation Gala. Please watch his acceptance speech. YouTube October 19th, 2018 - Realistic and heartwarming!

Eric, I cannot thank you enough- people like you give artists like me who are just starting as authors- the courage and the strength to keep writing- even though sometimes I feel my work is not that worthy - I can sometimes imagine you saying to me " Yes Lola just keep it going - never stop trying - believe in yourself. Let your voice be heard, you do make a difference in people's lives!" WOW - for this keeps me on track, writing fiercely and hopeful every day!

With Gratitude and Complete Admiration
Sincerely, Lola J Hobbs

Eric McCormack My Most Noble Gander ->

SPECIAL THANKS

To Tessla H - My angel. My sweetheart of a daughter. She makes me laugh every day. Reliable and always comes to my rescue. I am so very proud of her- she takes on the weight of the world and has been a blessing to our family.

To my sweet friend Lorrie D - We share a lot of stories between us about everything in our lives. A little bit of Madness mixed with Magic. I love the way she laughs! Lorrie is so positive and has made me a better person in many ways.

I especially enjoy her company, and she has amazing adorable dogs. She walks them to the dog park daily. We enjoy having lunch or dinner and watching movies together. Thank you so much for being my good friend and understanding me!

To Michelle A.- Thank you for being a good friend to me and my neighbor. Thank you so much for caring about me the way you do.

TABLE OF CONTENTS

Chapter 1. Favorite Quotes

Chapter 2. Pets

Chapter 3. Animals

Chapter 4. Religious

Chapter 5. Somewhat Dark

Chapter 6. Love

Peace.

It does not mean to be in a place where there is no noise, trouble or hard work. It means to be in the midst of those things and still be calm in your heart.

Unknown

FAVORITE QUOTES

"Stick with people who pull the magic out of you and not the madness."
-Unknown

Author comment: Exactly!

"I don't want to be part of a world for being kind as a weakness."
Credit: Keanu Reeves

Author comment: Kindness SHOULD be an easy-given part of any society. I believe this is a strength, not a weakness.

"The only person you are destined to become is the person you decide to be."
Credit: Ralph Waldo Emerson {1803-1882}

Author comment: Very true, often you must remind yourself.

"In order to be irreplaceable, one must always be different."
Credit: Coco Chanel, French Fashion designer {1883-1971}

Author comment - I am definitely different and I like myself for that!

"You got to lose to know how to win"
Credit: Song by Aerosmith, Dream On - Released 1973

Author comment: Hard Fact.

"Come forth into the light of things, let nature be your teacher."

"Your mind is your garden, your thoughts are your seeds, you can grow flowers or you can grow weeds."
Credit: William Wadsworth {1770-1850}

FAVORITE QUOTES

Author comment: Nature came into place when I discovered the wonderful Canada geese. Then those weeds became replaced by flowers.

"Life is worth living as long as there's a laugh in it"
Credit: L.M. Montgomery

Author comment: I only wish I thought like this when I was younger.

"Life is really simple but we insist on making it complicated." Confucius

Author comment: Exactly!

"Never forget the people who take the time out of their day to check up on you"
- Unknown

Author comment: Yes!

"I'm a rock I am an island and a rock feels no pain, and an island never cries"
Credit: I Am A Rock - Song by Simon and Garfunkel's - Released 1966

Author comment: I have felt much pain and cried too many tears.

"What doesn't kill you makes you stronger"
Credit: Stronger - Song by Kelly Clarkson - Released 2011

Author comment: I am grateful for those bad times because, they did make me stronger.

" Sometimes I feel like giving up no medicine is strong enough."

FAVORITE QUOTES

Credit: In My Blood - Song by Shawn Mendes - Released 2018 - About his own experiences with anxiety.

Author comment: Sometimes people just don't understand anxiety unless they have it themselves or a loved one that does.

"There is no greater wealth in this world than peace of mind."
Credit: Thoughts Wonder

Author comment: I do believe this is so true.

"A friend is someone who gives you total freedom to be yourself."
Credit: Jim Morrison - American singer-songwriter 1943-1971

Author comment - I especially adore the people who accept me as me.

"Sometimes you have to tell the negative committee in your mind to sit down and shut up." Credit: Ann Bradford.

Author comment - Yes, I constantly have to remind myself about that awful negative committee.

"I needed to hate you to love me, I needed to lose you to find me."

Credit: Lose You To Love Me - Song by Selena Gomez - Released 2020

Author comment: Wow can I relate to this - It took me quite a while to figure this out after I left my only true love.

FAVORITE QUOTES

"Insanity is doing the same thing over and over again expecting different results." Credit: Albert Einstein 1879-1955

Author comment: Yes there was a time when I would not have understood this.

"Try not to become a man of success, But rather a man of value." Credit: Albert Einstein 1879 -1955

PETS

Gorgeous kitties enjoying a view from my living room window. Oliver, Toby and Marvin - all rescues, they keep each other company and play together often. They have taken over my home!

Photo credit: Amy I.

Adorable poodle mix - 17 years old - rescued from True Blue Pet Rescue at 12 years old. By Colleen B. Taking a rest in tne sun. He is very sweet and mellow. The dog that everybody loves!

Photo credit: Matt

PETS

Nerdy: A Maine Coon kitten that was rescued from Aurora Animal Shelter. He especially loved to be carried around in a frontal baby carrier. One day I was fiercely working on my computer, for many hours. Then suddenly, Nerdy jumped up and peed all over my keyboard. He quickly jumped off. As he proudly walked away, I swear he was smirking and thinking to himself haha I killed it!

Photo credit: Nancy F.

Tux: A tuxedo kitten that was quickly rescued by a sweet family. He was left by an awful family who moved and just left him on the streets. Tux is very friendly and meows a lot- especially 20 minutes before mealtime, he loves people and always wants to be pet. His vocal cords are strong. He is handsome and he knows it, he struts around the house, with his tail in the air, like he doesn't care.

Photo credit: Tyler H.

PETS

Von - A 7-year-old purebred red Doberman from South Carolina. He is extremely intelligent. He does not like when people use their phones, either texting or talking he starts barking at them, in other words, get off the phone and pay attention to me! Von is very gentle with the cats in the home.

Photo credit: Tessla H.

Mia - A 12-year-old Shih Tzu who loves to play ball and adores her daddy Tyler. She is so well trained, she stays right by Daddy and doesn't need a leash.

Photo credit: Lola

PETS

Vinny - My 13-year-old schnauzer - was the love of my life- we walked everywhere together and he truly adored me. Vinny was a rescue and he had been severely abused. I am happy that I was able to give the last years of his life- the happiest years. He will forever be in my heart. I miss you madly every day.

Photo credit: Lola

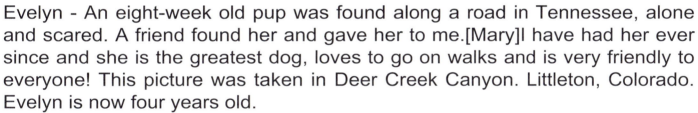

Evelyn - An eight-week old pup was found along a road in Tennessee, alone and scared. A friend found her and gave her to me.[Mary]I have had her ever since and she is the greatest dog, loves to go on walks and is very friendly to everyone! This picture was taken in Deer Creek Canyon. Littleton, Colorado. Evelyn is now four years old.

Photo credit: Mary K.

PETS

Azules - This Kitty was a mixture of Siamese and Maltese. We acquired him as a kitten when some teenagers sold him outside of King Soopers for $5. We named him Azules because of his blue eyes. He was an adorable fun Kitty who loved to eat, therefore he became quite chubby. So we nicknamed him Booboo. When he walked around the house he talked an awful lot, he was so charming. We all miss you so much Booboo.

Photo credit: Tessla H.

Lilly and Coco: Lilly is 7 years old now - Coco is 10 months old. They're good friends and soul sisters who occasionally fight over the same dog bed. They love going on walks together and are great companions.

Photo credit: Lorrie D.

ANIMALS

Hello, I am Mama Goose. This photo is of me and my goslings. As soon as I am aware I'm pregnant, I work non-stop to build a nest. I form the outside with twigs or moss, then I lay my body on the ground move it around and make an indention. After that, I pluck the down from my body to make a cushion for the nest. It will take at least one and a half days for me to lay each egg. Then I must keep my warm body on the nest for 28 days, I rotate the eggs often and with my beak. I will sit there all day and night through rain, hail, gusty winds, and snow storms.

Once they hatch, my young ones sit underneath my wings to keep warm. They are exceptionally sweet. My son decided to rest on my back [as you can see in this photo] and he is extremely curious already. This one's going to become rambunctious quickly!

I will decide that that first day is exciting as I will lead them down to the lake for their first swim, my little ones will follow me and, my mate the Gander, will follow behind keeping me, watching out for any predators and protecting us, he is proud and daring. I love him so much we are mates for life.

The Ducks are often seen hanging out with us. Sometimes the mother duck will build a nest to mine. We think those ducklings are cute too. We respect them. They are waterfowl and are similar to us in many ways. Except they quack and we honk.

I love my children just like any other mother, they mean the world to me, and I live mostly just for them. They follow closely to me everywhere. They watch my every move. My mate protects us, he will fight to the death for us. I believe that makes us sort of like you humans, am I right?

ANIMALS

Although humans are delighted to see my babies when they are young and little adorable things, soon they will grow up and look just like me, they will double their size every week, just from eating plenty of grass. Sadly, that's when some of you don't like my babies anymore.

Unfortunately, because of our strange digestive system, we poop often, this digestive system is set up in a way that we do not urinate. I'm sorry for this, it's offensive to most humans but I do understand. Also for many of the pet owners, this has become a huge problem. For this, I am sincerely sorry. I say this with compassion, we are highly emotional like most of you.

You see we're intelligent birds. Have you ever seen us flying in a V-formation? This takes plenty of practice and discipline! I am deeply disturbed by the inconvenience we cause you and your pets. Except, please try to be sympathetic towards us. We have been forced out of many of our homes. While humans are busy building plenty of projects everywhere, a lot of wildlife is being forced out.

We are still determining where the other animals are going to live to survive. We are concerned about them, are you? Most likely you are yet unfortunately there's not much we can do is there?

As geese, we have discovered parks and golf courses with lakes that we love to swim in and eat grass for nourishment. Therefore that's where we go. We don't have a choice, so please forgive us.

I'm pleading with you, don't hate us! We like to form groups together and raise our young to play with all the other geese' families, we enjoy their company. Again, I feel like we are a lot like humans in this way too.

ANIMALS

We are grateful for the people who like us and will definitely remember kind humans. Every living thing on this earth has as much of a right to be here as you do!

Love from Mama Goose.

DUCKS

A pair of ducks swimming in St. Petersburg, Florida
Photo credit: Huyla M.

JACKIE

Jackie is a very special stuffed unicorn - she is my favorite friend
She's so beautiful with a teal body - sparkles - pink fringe and a pink tail
She always keeps me company - Jackie always makes me feel better

My sweet miracle - My home is a better place with her presence
Jackie sleeps on my bed every night
During the day - She sits on my desk - while I'm at school

When I get home I softly hug her
She inspires me to have fun which in turn - makes me a better person
She sits beside me while I do my homework
She watches me when I help Mom make dinner

When I play music in my room - she dances with me

She loves the sounds of my bopping music
Jackie loves me for who I am - she doesn't want to change me
She thinks I'm Funny - she thinks I'm Fantastic

Jackie understands how I feel - She's real to me

My friends think I'm a freak because - I like her so much - those jerks!
Well honestly - She is better than most people
She loves me back and she doesn't judge me

I can be myself around her - I dance - I laugh - I
sing I ultimately always enjoy my time with Jackie
So what's wrong with that? Nothing!
Yeah that's right - I'm a Rockstar!

A GOSLING

Hi there - I am a 3-month-old girl gosling - I was born by the golf course at Heather Gardens - This is my story:

I broke my leg climbing over those awful huge rocks trying to get into the lake with my family - then they left me - I have been crying and swimming around looking for them for days on end.

I don't know why they stopped loving me or why they left me. All I know is I miss them terribly - Mom, Dad my two sisters, and my brother. I need my family - I'm just a baby!

I can swim pretty well - I get out upon the rocks sometimes it's difficult but I know I have to eat the grass - my parents taught me that.

Then one very hot August day - these people came along- one of the ladies had this huge net - she was fast - caught me and then I jumped OUT into the water and swam to the other side. Why is she trying to catch me?

Maybe she's going to take me to my family - WOW ! That would be great. I swam around for about 20 minutes - then I got hungry - so I crawled out off the rocks- to have a snack on some grass - this lady her name[I found out was Cory] she caught me with that net again!

This time a man named AK gently put a towel over me - I thought it was - so I could not see what was going on and that I wouldn't be scared- then these ladies named Lola and Jen gently put me into a carrier- it was pink - I was very frightened - except I thought they were going to take me to see my family. Do they know where they are?

A GOSLING

I was certain they did - of course they do. It turned out all these people were very kind. I heard them saying this - we must get her to a rescue as soon as possible so they could fix her broken leg. Lola and AK put me into a car and Lola held me on her lap In the carrier - she spoke to me softly and told me everything was going to be okay.

She said - I have named you Josie. You see I have extremely keen hearing - I could tell - she was crying - then I started crying because I thought that I wasn't going to see my family. Oh No, I hope this cannot be true! I am terribly scared I felt sick In my stomach.

After quite a long drive, we arrived at this place - the girls were very friendly and they took me into the back - again I thought my family would be there but they weren't. They handled me very carefully and spoke to me sweetly.

I could tell they cared about me - lots of kind people I met today. I heard them say that my leg was badly broken and I would need surgery right away. Whatever that is - I'm scared again! I went to sleep and when I woke up I had a big bandage on my leg and it felt weird and tight. I was so tired, except the girls at the hospital took really good care of me. They gave me water- some food I never had before. I have only eaten grass - but they gave me mixed corn, oats, and delicious sweet berries. WOW!

A GOSLING

I heard them say she's going to stay with us for a couple of months - then she'll be strong. Everyone there took extremely good care of me - they all made me feel so special - always calling me Josie - I like that name! I got medicine every day and I didn't feel any pain. I felt safe there.

After my bandage came off they gave me a small pool to swim in. Sometimes I still missed my family - I wondered, are they looking for me? Then-one day the girls put me in a carrier and took me for a drive. They opened my cage and let me outside to this beautiful place with trees, a lake with other families of geese just like me! I immediately flew onto the water.

It felt so good that I quickly swam over to this nice family and the Mama goose looked at me with a gleam in her eyes and swam close to me. I told her my name was Josie. Then I joined her family I was so incredibly happy - I swam along the lake together with the other young geese - I felt warm and fuzzy inside. The bright sun was shining on my feathers - I was excited and never felt alone again. AMAZING! My new family loved me like their own.

This is a true story: The afternoon that this incident took place at Heather Gardens Golf Course on a busy Sunday with golfers - some people asked what was going on - we told them we were going to take this poor gosling to a special hospital to save her- this occurrence took about 45 minutes - the golfers stopped golfing- many people were watching on the bridge area - when Josie was finally rescued by us - the group of people was cheering and clapping! We did not notice the crowd that had gathered.

A GOSLING

We were truly impressed by the compassion that these people had shown! Josie was taken to the Rocky Mountain Wild Alliance rescue in Sedalia - after X-rays were observed. We were told that they would do everything to help Josie with her badly broken leg. When she was strong enough to fly - the remarkable employees took her to a body of water approximately 10 miles from the place where she was found.

Our dear Josie - you will always remain a fond memory in our hearts. We are thrilled that you are healthy and happy with your new family.

Love from Lola, Jen, Cory, and AK.

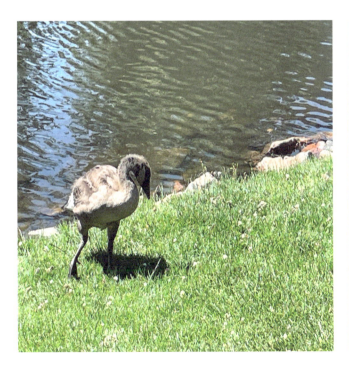

JACOB

    Hello there - my name is Jacob
I am a 2- year old Canada goose { a gander}
It's a hot July day in Colorado
You see I am different from all the others
I have an awful deformed leg- It's ugly
I am a threat to the other geese and goslings
I am easy prey for the fox and the coyotes that run along the lakes here

    Where I live - actually it's where I survive - Yes I keep to myself
I am an outcast - therefore I'm so sad all the time
I will never have a mate - the other Ganders are happy
They have mates for life - Cute wives
So Their Main Purpose is to defend them - and the babies too - Hiss-Honk
The other male geese peck at me - chase me away - so mean
It's not my fault I Was Born This Way with an ugly twisted leg
The leg doesn't hurt - I can even walk on it - with a lean

    Today I sat under the tree to get some shade from the 93° weather
Staring at the lake just wishing I could go in there for a drink - for a swim
Except I'm afraid of the other ganders - Why are the so mean?
Some people passing by - gave me a few of the crap apples
They picked from the tree - especially for me - very kind
Those people see me alone every day - they always look my way
I hear them speaking about me - I look sad - they say

    I wonder if I was a human just for a day
What it would be like - to play with other kids
Swim in a pool - drink - juice boxes- eat cookies-yum

JACOB

     I dream about this at night - when I sometimes sleep
The Fright of the Predators prancing - so quietly
So eager to grab - Gobble me up

     I have been lucky in that way - Or am I? Not
Then the next day - it starts over again
My sadness sinks in - NONE of the other geese want to be my friend
They chase me away - I feel like the enemy
I have no purpose - All these feathers and down - I feel so hot
I sit under the tree - not much shade when it's 93°

     A sweet lady came by - took a picture of me
She said with a crackle in her voice - The sun is Bright
Oh Jacob please go down to the water - Don't be afraid
You are hot and thirsty - as I sat so still
I saw tears run down her face - she cried and walked away
If I was human - I could be her son - HURRAY!

     I would laugh - play - drink juice boxes - eat snacks - all day
She would protect me in every way
I am just a goose - I will survive this
As Good As It Gets?
Except - maybe my loneliness is getting the best of me

     Today I was alone by the crabapple tree - tasty treats
I spotted someone walking a big dog
So I honked and honked as loud as I could - warning all the other
geese I felt like a Hero for a moment there - yet still they did not care
I may not see tomorrow - because I am an easy game

JACOB

    For that Vicious Hungry Predator
Will it even matter? I'm just another pesty goose anyway
I do believe that many of those kind - people could miss me

    Author's note: After watching Jacob daily he suddenly disappeared. Since this happened I thought it would be better that I didn't name the geese - maybe I won't get so attached to them or is this possible for me?

Photo: By Lola - Goose at the Heather Gardens Golf Course - July 2023
This gander is preening himself after a swim in the lake - Notice his broken leg is just hanging there.

THE ROOSTER

Hello, my name is Lucy.
We lived in a cute ranch house in Wallingford Connecticut. I didn't have any pets so I played with my baby and Barbie dolls, they were my best company.

Summers were hot and humid. My neighbors had a fantastic pool that I enjoyed swimming in. I was good friends with Sally, she was my age and we went to school together. Her parents were rich. They were always friendly and kind to me.

Sometimes Sally would come over and play with me on my swing set. I didn't have all the toys that she had, so we would read books together. We did homework at my house right after school.

Then one day a nice man came along while she was outside watering our tulips. He asked my mom to take his rooster because unfortunately, the man couldn't keep him anymore. This rooster was young and we named him Chic-Chic. He was so loud in the morning!

My dad worked pretty late, so Mom and I used to have dinner around 5:00 and Chick-Chick would sit on the chair right by us and she fed him human food all the time. He was funny in the way he would strut around the house, he was our only pet. I really wanted a kitty, oh well.

Mom especially loved this rooster - except Sally's parents did not!
They complained to my dad and said we had no right having him, after all, we didn't live on a farm and his crowing in the morning annoyed them.

THE ROOSTER

We drove to the country and found a farm that was excited to have Chick-Chick, he was strong and healthy. They told us they would take very good care of him.

I had a great time visiting this farm. They had horses, sheep, goats, chickens, pigs, cows and geese. I loved petting the animals I wanted to live there forever.

The teenager that lived there named Cyndi took me around. She told me that she was responsible for helping take care of all the animals. Cyndi said "We are vegetarians and we never kill any of our animals. They are pets to us."

"My family grows all our vegetables." Then she showed me their huge vegetable area which went for miles and miles. It was fantastic and there were many flowers among them.

I had so much fun I didn't want to leave. This sweet family told us we could come back anytime and gave my parents their phone number.

I knew that Chick-Chick would have a great life there. Except my mom cried all the way home. I felt so sorry for her I wish I could fix it.

We visited the farm almost every weekend and had dinner there with this incredible family that adored Chick-Chick among all the other pets. He stayed in a chicken coop at night and got to run around during the day.

This fantastic farm also had three Australian Cattle Dogs. These dogs were the protectors. They were fast and very alert to what was going on at every moment.

THE ROOSTER

I've been a vegetarian ever since then, there's no way I'm going to eat any meat ever again! I love animals so much. My parents were okay with this. I packed my lunch every day myself. They were proud of me.

Although my mom was distraught over losing her rooster, she wasn't angry at Sally's parents, she understood how loud he was in the morning.

I was concerned about this as Sally was my best friend. She wasn't a snob even though they had a lot of money. I was happy that she valued our friendship.

My dad set up a tent in our backyard and we played dolls in there. My Mom finally stopped crying - except for what seemed like forever!

You never want to see your mom sad - never ever! I have a fantastic imagination, so sometimes I make up silly plays and she laughs. It was great to see her smiling.

NATE

NATE: This lone gander was roaming around looking for his mate and sadly crying for her. I got a little closer to get a pic of him- so he fiercely swam into the water. This photo was taken at the office buildings on South Vaughn Way.

FEFE

FEFE: I spotted this goose looking out over the lake for her lost mate. Although the geese are mates for life - sometimes they could get lost especially during the migrating time. She is sad and lonely. As I sat on a bench at the Heather Gardens Golf Course she came next to me and slept for awhile.

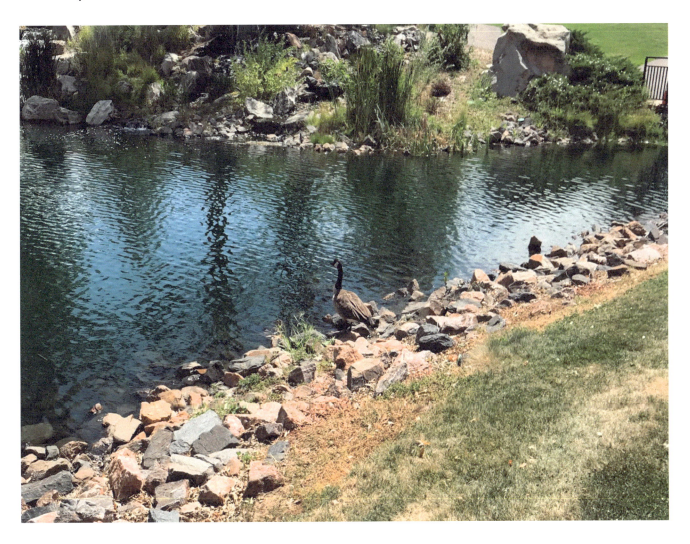

To My Precious Canada Geese

    It is Springtime in the Rockies
You are my favorite distraction from the world we live in now
When I visit you at the nearby lake
I love that - I lose any notion of time

    Now you have goslings- so adorable you make my heart sing
Sets of eight, six, five, four and three…
I walked by to get a good video of Mama {goose}
And the {Daddy} gander hiss-his-hiss

    Of course - I must include those darling goslings
Yet I keep my distance - I am respectful
Gander - you are so brave and protect your mate and your little ones
Gander - you will fight until the death to protect your family.

    People walking by adore you - when you are the small cute little
goslings Soon you will be grown - I still feel you are Heavenly
Some ignorant people feel you are now pesty
I will always see you as Beautiful and Delightful
Precious - Strong - Compassionate birds

    Your Family - Friends of your flock-are everything to you and more
Your goose world is filled with compassion
Therefore you are so much more human than some people

MR. AND MRS.

    A gander flies into the lake stopping fiercely with his feet
Aha - he now awaits patiently for her return
Not swimming - just floating-waiting
Suddenly he starts calling for his mate - honk! honk! honk!

    Very loud and a high-pitched cry
I've heard that cry many times before
I sat there on the park bench just watching and waiting
Wishing she would come along soon

    Mates for life - they treasure each other
As the pretty green leaves from the tree in front of me
Sway ever so lightly from the breeze - I look up to the sky

    She recognizes his call- So quickly - she flies into the lake
Excited to meet her mate she almost collides into him
Quite a funny yet lovely sight to see
They swim together for a while closely side by side

    Mr. and Mrs. get out of the water
Walks across the rocks onto the grass
They waddle happily off to the sunset
Sweetly, the couple takes a rest together.

MR. AND MRS.

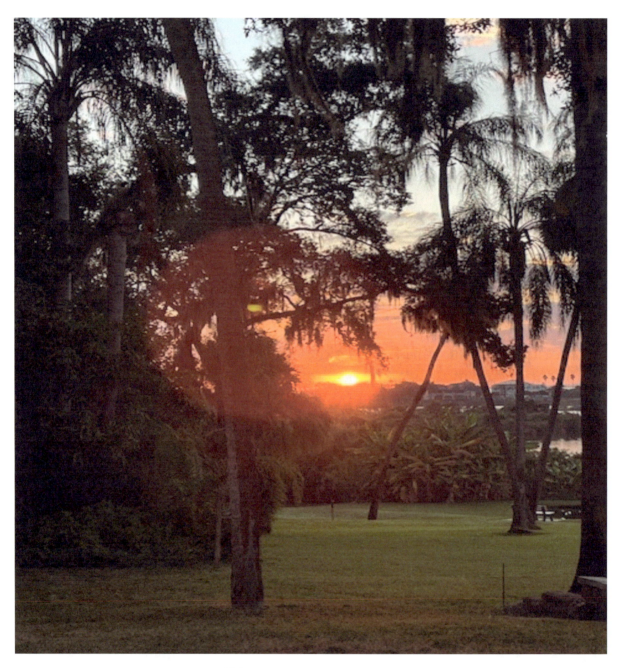

Photo credit: Nancy F.

CARDINAL

Cardinals are found most of the time in - Arizona California - New Mexico - New York - Florida and New England.

Most couples stay together - the young baby Cardinals are pretty demanding the first few days after they have hatched - their parents feed them up to eight times per hour! Feeding them spiders and insects they also get their liquids from the foods they eat.

Cardinals are considered to represent lost loved ones. Giving us a sign that we are on the right path and they are caring and watching over us.

WILL AND GRACE

Will and Grace: My favorite TV comedy series… Will, as he's flapping his wings and turns his back in frustration says with an angry voice: "Grace, you left your feathers all over the shower drain again! You are so irresponsible and selfish! Grace, why oh why? Can you PLEASE stop doing this?"

Grace shouts: "Oh, there you go again with your controlling issues. Just get over it, and I mean this Will, I'm leaving to get a pizza and I'm going to eat the WHOLE thing myself!" HA!

Photo credit: Lola

BARRY AND HARRY

It was a very quiet early spring morning in a large park. A beautiful sunrise rose upon the crystal blue lake and flowers were blooming everywhere.

A lonely snow goose was quickly hobbling along a path as fast as he could, he kept looking side to side, he seemed lost and a bit frantic.

Out of nowhere, a cute orange tabby kitten appeared. "Oh, hello there, said the kitten, my name is Barry, what is your name?"

"Yeah, my name is Harry". He was in a huge rush and was quite annoyed by Barry, who was an extremely curious, chatty orange tabby kitten with plenty of questions. Barry asked," Where are you going in such a hurry?" "I MUST find my flock Harry shouted!"

BARRY AND HARRY

"Can I help you find them?" Barry replied," I'm very good at finding things, you would be one hundred percent surprised."

Harry did not want Barry or anyone else around except his lost flock of geese, so he shouted at Barry again. "NO-NO you must go away go away you pesty little kitten!"

Harry wanted to get far away from Barry except the snow goose walked with terrible hobble while the kitten walked quickly. Barry repeated, "Can I help you find them, I'm very good at finding things?

Then something terrible happened, Barry began to cry big tears, the tears flooding down down all over Harry's big orange webbed feet.

"Now- now- don't be sad, yes you can help me find my flock, it's going to require us walking all over this park hopefully, this won't take too long." Barry agreed and thought it would be a great adventure.

Suddenly, the sky opened and started raining excessive huge raindrops. Harry swaddled Barry under his wing and walked him underneath a tree, they sat there together waiting for the rain to pass. Finally, the rain stopped. A gigantic sun burst out from the bright blue sky and a beautiful rainbow appeared.

As they continued walking up each path of the park, animals started coming out from everywhere. An aggressive squirrel came running up to Barry and scared him. Harry let out a loud " HONK! HONK! HONK! The squirrel fiercely ran up onto a tree.

BARRY AND HARRY

Then a large bunny came hopping all over and scared Barry. Harry let out another loud" HONK! HONK! HONK!" the bunny quickly hopped away into a bush. Abruptly a dog came running up to Barry, this time Harry flapped his wings and the dog swiftly ran away!

"Wow you are so brave, are we good friends now?" Harry was amazed that anyone thought he was brave, he had NEVER been told that before. He answered with a crackling voice, "Yes of course we are good friends, but only until I find my flock, and then I will be flying away with them. You can finally return to your home. I am sure your family is looking for you, a little kitten should not be roaming around the park alone."

Again, Barry began to cry big tears, flowing down all over Harry's big orange webbed feet. "I don't have a home anymore, you see I think my family moved away and left me behind I have waited for days and days on end hoping for their return, that they might be on vacation, but they never came back for me. A bowl of water and some food were left outside.

I only lived inside the house and I never went outside, I became lonely. So I just started walking around the park, then when I saw you and you looked lonely too, I just thought that snow goose could maybe become my friend."

Larry and Barry continued their search for Harry's flock they looked up into the sky and saw kites flying and a few ducks except no geese, not a single goose in sight. Barry became worried.

Harry became extremely sad, he just sat down on the grass and tucked his head into his chest, Barry licked Harry's head to comfort him.

BARRY AND HARRY

"Don't be sad Harry, we will find your flock okay? How did you lose them anyhow? Why do you walk with such an awful limp? How old are you? {this kitten was inquisitive under any circumstances}

So Harry proceeded to tell Barry about his story…" I'm three years old now, you see I'm not that old. I was born with a limp, I am a cripple, and the other male geese always taunt and tease me. None of the female geese will pick me as a mate. If only I could meet a nice lady goose who would see that I was kind, gentle, intelligent, and a great protector. I feel like that day will never come.

Today I was with my flock, I went to eat some grass by a nearby tree, and when I turned around all the other geese were gone, they just left me, I'm afraid they might have done this on purpose. I'm not accepted by them and that's mean."

The snow goose and the curious kitten had something in common, they were both abandoned. Barry wanted to make Harry feel better, but he was nervous so he just started chattering. "My favorite food is fish I just love fish I don't know where to find them. I just love fish I can't wait to find some fish, and have a feast. I'm so hungry!"

Harry looked at Barry with a sparkle in his eyes. "Aha, so you love fish do you?" he became very amused and was immediately thrilled.

Instantly, Harry thought of a great idea, for he was a courageous and creative snow goose. "Get up onto my back he told Barry."

"Why oh why? Where are we going? What are we doing?"

BARRY AND HARRY

"You'll see it's a surprise, you curious adorable kitten, please trust me, my good friend." Barry was astonished to hear that he was Harry's good friend. Excited and fearless he climbed onto Harry's back. The snow goose flew open his wings. They went high up into the sky. The kitten wasn't afraid and lonely anymore.

As they went over pastures of green grass. Barry looked below and saw a lake with fish jumping all over. YUM! He spotted a pretty lady snow goose swimming alone on the lake and thought." She's going to love Harry now that he isn't a grumpy old goose anymore."

Harry and Barry safely landed on the grass, near the lake. To his surprise, a sweet girl kitten walked toward him. The lady snow goose, came out of the water and simply waddled over to Harry. They were all beaming with happiness.

This became a purr-fect place they both could call home.

ADORABLE GEESE FAMILY

I snapped this photo at Heather Gardens golf course in June of 2023.

MATES FOR LIFE

    March 2023 - It was a lovely sunny day - at Heather Gardens golf course
A gander walking so fast taking - great big steps I wondered why is he in
such a frenzy? I named him Ray - He got into the water and started
honking loudly

    I know that call - a lonely high-pitched screech
He was looking for his mate - soon seven new geese - flew onto the other
side of the lake

    Ray was excited - so away he paddled those webbed feet
quickly-underneath the nearby bridge

    To meet up with the other geese - I watch with dismay
Only to see him get brutally attacked by one of them
He desperately fought back with his wings sadly he swims away
She wasn't with them - too bad - so heartbroken

    Ray - I hope you find her today as I shed a tear
These lonely geese become easily depressed - they are highly emotional

                      Always Mates For Life

FREE TO BE ME

    Tess is a Canada goose who lives - along a beautiful riverbank
She is about - two and a half years old
Her favorite thing to do - is swim in the smooth cool river

    She uses her huge webbed feet- advantage to swim
Around the lake - splashing - going underwater - brillant back flips
One group is - other single female geese - her age

FREE TO BE ME

Another group - single male geese - about 3 years old
Her girlfriends were kind - SOME of the time
ALWAYS keeping their feathers impeccable
They just can't wait - for that first date
Extremely EAGER to find - perfect mate

They often flirt with - the many single Gentleman geese
Looking for that special one to become - their mate for life
He must be strong - Best to protect - Eager to fight predators - In every way - So the Gents exhibit many displays - Everyday

Yes- they entertain - fighting each other - seriously - yet playful ?
Just knowing those - Adorable Ladies are looking their way
Except for Tess - she just swims all-day

Trish asks Tess - Why are you this way?
Fix your feathers - You look a mess - an absolute disgrace
There are so many boys - just wanting to play
We get to choose - who will be our mate - isn't that great?

No Trish - I don't want a mate - I don't want babies
I'd rather swim - dive - do things my way - FREE TO BE ME
I don't need a mate - You see - I'm happy - just fine

Oh no -no -no- All the lady geese squawked- you're just crazy and lazy
Maybe look again- over there-across the river
So many sexy boys - How could you not feel their erotic vibes?
Just flowing our way?

FREE TO BE ME

Tabitha was the most dazzling lady goose
Flaunted that waddle - as she walked - sending off flares
All those gents - would stop - stare - glare
None of the other lady geese - could compare

Tabitha suggested - with a snicker - Tess - be the first one to pick a mate
Go ahead - giggled the Ladies - which gent do you fancy?
Tess looked for awhile - across the glossy river
She shook her head - no - no - no!

All the lady geese - were somewhat - amused - confused
What will you do without a mate?
Tess exclaimed - I shall spread my wings - fly far-far away
The very next day - after - an extremely long swim

Tess finally- precisely - cleaned all her feathers - magnificent
WOW! She looked stunning - Is she going to pick her mate TODAY? Eagerly -
ALL the Canada Geese - watched anxiously
To their dismay - SUDDENLY - she just flew away

Tess flapped her wings quickly -just all alone
Looking for the perfect place- a single Island
With no one around- only the sound of the water- against the pebbly sand
After miles and miles- she spotted a single Island-Paradise

This is a place to stay forever - with berry bushes galore
Tess had a wonderful lunch - she rested beneath a fig tree
In the shade - For a couple of days - Yep this is the life that I want
Finally - I'M FREE TO BE ME- no one telling me what to do or look pretty for

FREE TO BE ME

Oh yes - this will do just fine - excellent choice I must say
She jumped off the island - swam into clear blue water
Splashing - having a great time - hours on end
Then went back to sleep under - the perfect fig tree
Dreaming - Splendid- Days Ahead

The sound of ruffles - among the green leaves above
Abruptly woke her up - Who could this be? - I thought I was free!
I want to be alone - this island is just for me

Tess was sleepy - yet greatly disturbed
She heard these loud sounds - A funny looking thing
Up in the tree - extraordinary bird -bright colors - much shorter wings
Chomping on figs - Some fell below - hitting Tess - right on her head

Hey there excuse me! What are you? Why are you here?
Good morning - my dear - My name is Tiff
I am a parrot - I came here to be alone - FREE TO BE ME
I don't swim - just sit in a tree - most of the day

Clean my beautiful feathers - or stray along the shore
What is your name? - Are those berries yummy?
My name is Tess - Oh those berries are - the best
Tiff asked - can we be friends - just You and Me?

Tess was reluctant - to say anything - she was not happy with the visitor
Maybe - I should just ignore her - She'll go away
Then something in her heart - changed her mind
She remembered she was kind - not like those lady geese - she left behind

FREE TO BE ME

Sure - said Tess - Please - don't invite ANYONE else - no ladies - no gents
Oh no no - I wouldn't dare - PERFECT- just the two of us -a secret ONLY we share Berries - figs - Wonderful Sunshine - Warm sand - Peacefulness
EXCEPT - You see - I talk - a lot - That's what Parrots do
Tess explained - no worries my dear
I'll be swimming - close by - In the clear blue water
So - Just the two of them - continuously laughing - together
Tess swam - splashed - all day
While Tiff - chattered away
All you need is one good friend - To spend every day
Who lifts you up in every way

As a member of The Humane Society I feel very passionate about animal rights.

RELIGIOUS

I went last-minute Christmas shopping today. It's 5 days before Christmas and I decided to go to Walmart. I've been working a lot and that's the only excuse I can come up with right now.

All at once, it starts snowing. Well, that's Colorado for you one minute the sun's out, and the next minute you're in a blizzard. I can't believe I'm here at Walmart no less - there were no parking places, and it was packed. I swear I think I might have parked in another state. At this point, I was in horrific confusion.

I went into the store full of people, there was no room to walk actually. As I pushed my rickety cart around everybody was extremely grouchy. No need to make eye contact. I felt just the same, I was furious with myself. "What am I doing in this Walmart 5 days before Christmas?" I was speaking out loud to myself, who cares at this point?

I needed some decorations to put on the front of the door, in my new apartment. So how am I going to get through all these people? What am I doing at Walmart five days before Christmas? I was furious, as I made my way around a corner and spotted some gift bags oh yeah I need some of these of course I do, or do I?

Yes, I was completely delirious. The Christmas music was blasting on the intercom, not too many stores do that anymore. I do enjoy music, except today, which was sort of annoying. So I shoveled my way with my raggedy cart up to the section with the gift bags there were a few left, and that's what happens when you leave the shopping until the last minute.

RELIGIOUS

As I was looking at the small selection of bags, I stood there for a moment, for some unknown reason I looked to my left... on the end corner of a shelf amongst the mess of ribbons, bags, tags, a few stockings and some Christmas paper, was a statue, she was looking right at me! I looked around to see if there were any other items in this area, that somewhat looked like her. There wasn't any. There she was, this precious 11th angel, just alone.

It was like she was standing there just for me- I mean somebody left her there obviously, amongst the mess of bags and whatnot.

They decided not to buy her - except seriously - she was graciously looking right at me. I went over and gently picked her up. I shouted - "This is WHY I'm here 5 days before Christmas in a Walmart!" The store was so loud and crazy! Nobody cared that I had become somewhat insane- in a good way? I looked her over to see if she had any cracks or chips on her except she was perfect!

It wouldn't matter if she had not been perfect. I turned her over to see the price of $11.99 -for decoration only. I was so happy that someone had left her there among that extraordinary mess, she's a blessing. I picked her up and held her close to me, got the few things that I had - left that old raggedy cart, and went immediately to the checkout.

The lines were hideous. Except this was glorious. I found an 11th Angel for my new apartment and I wasn't even looking for her - she was MEANT for me. MERRY CHRISTMAS!

RELIGIOUS

After making it through the checkout lane, I made sure I found some cash to put into the Salvation Army bucket outside the door with the faithful bell ringer. He smiled and said thank you, even though he must have been freezing from the cold weather.

I carefully brought her home and she sits in my living room and watches over me. That's what I was doing in a Walmart five days before Christmas! Unbelievable! I love my 11th Angel. By the way, I didn't find any decorations for my door and it didn't matter. Amen.

RELIGIOUS

You don't need to be born talented to be creative!

Ideas last forever - I love my fairytale world.

May today bring you Joy, Love, Peace and, all the blessings your heart can possibly hold!

May God bless you today and everyday and everyone you love and, everything you love!

Time is like a river… you cannot touch the same water twice - because the flow that has passed will never pass again. Enjoy every moment of your life!

Smiles warm the heart: they are contagious! This may take practice - just give peace a chance.

Be humble - be happy!

Remember being happy doesn't mean you have it all… it simply means you're thankful for what you have.

Always be kind - be sensitive to others- you never know what someone else is going through! Amen.

I may not be where I want to be but thank God I'm not where I used to be.

Amen.

RELIGIOUS

Photo credit: Heather Gardens Chapel

RELIGIOUS QUOTES

"Start doing what's necessary; Then do what's possible, and suddenly you're doing the impossible." Credit: St. Francis of Assisi [1181-1226]
Author comment: I follow this daily

"I may not be where I want to be but thank God I'm not where I used to be."
Credit: Joyce Meyers
Author comment: I thank God every day for this!

"The Lord that I serve says that the impossible is unacceptable."
Credit: Stevie Wonder
Author comment: I couldn't agree more!

"Above all else, guard your heart for everything you do flows from it."
Proverbs 4:23

"Don't have a limited mindset. There's nothing more powerful than a changed mind" Credit: Joel Olsteen
Author comment: When I changed my mindset, doors opened.

"For God so loved the world, that he gave his only begotten Son, that whoever believeth in Him, should not perish, but have everlasting life."
John 3:16

"Faith is to believe what you do not see; the reward of this faith is to see what you believe" Credit: Saint Augustine

"I am the Good Shepherd.
The Good Shepherd gives his life for the Sheep."
John 10:11

SOMEWHAT DARK

Darkness sets in as I fall upon you, yet I haven't hit the ground.

Photo credit: Trenton S.

SOMEWHAT DARK

Hello anxiety - I see you are here to visit me again

Are you my frustrating friend who won't go away?

I've asked you not to stay - I don't like feeling this way

No, it's not okay it's not okay - even though

Sometimes that's what people say

I'm extremely exhausted from you

Visiting me every damn hour of each and every day

Just go away! I can't function properly this way

You are cramping my style - you are giving me headaches

Stomach aches, and heartaches I've suffered long enough from you!

It's just not something I can keep going through - I can't control you

I seriously hate you! Hate Is a word I don't like to use

See what you're doing to me?

PLEASE go away permanently - thank you!

From, Someone With An Attitude

SOMEWHAT DARK

Why Did I Love You

You noticed me - went after me like prey
Why did you think you were here to save my day?
Then I felt the danger - warning signs
Sadly - I was so hungry to be loved
Ultimately vulnerable - Just what you sought

You became charming - alluring - hypnotizing
Your flattering words - gave me sensitive attention
Then I was quickly swept off my feet
Bravely choose to put my fragile heart in your hands
Fascinated - the attraction was flaming hot
This drove me wild - except I felt like an innocent child

Even though I felt that danger - that irresistible energy you sent me
Yet I couldn't help myself - I had never met a man so dignified
Ignored those red flags-excessive drinking- gambling-dressed to impress
Nevertheless, soon-we became best friends
Will you be here till the end? I caught the fever - it was scary
In the back of my mind - I thought will he always be this kind?

Then - I put you first above everything you adored it
Was not sure what would happen next
This quickly turned into the most incredible sex
Yes I'll be that freak - you can taunt me - no rules

I couldn't wait to see you again - the wrenching anticipation
You felt the same way about me is what you said

SOMEWHAT DARK

Why Did I Love You

The thrilling meetups almost every day - just heartbeats away
We exchanged our vows of love - I LOVE YOU - I LOVE YOU TOO
I felt the angels singing above - makes sense - so intense
Yes, I'm naive - Is that why you chose me?
I'm in love and happy - nothing will ever take this away

Giving you everything I had - You became - glad - never mad
I was certain this would last forever - Leaps and Bounds of Trust
Such a dashing actor - who's in your head now? My entire body is worn
Is she in your arms when you're not with me? I feel absolutely torn
You were extremely clever - No one else ever sees your dark side
All the writing was on the wall - [spooky]
Including red hearts with blood dripping down

THE GAMES YOU PLAYED - THE GAMES YOU PLAYED

Not sure when - I became your favorite victim
Abusive beatings - Gaslighting - Are we both insane?
My constant crying gave you more power- Now I'm weak
You Damn Dream Crusher! My world is lonely and bleak
I was not aware - You were a maladaptive Narcissist

Now you are a Vampire - draining all my blood
And as the Devil laughing - you stole my soul
How did your love turn to hate? This is a trick not fate
What's happening - is this some sort of a hit-and-run?
My brain is mush - I'm confused - Why did I love you?

SOMEWHAT DARK

Why Did I Love You

Thought of leaving then suddenly - I was frozen
Then when I stayed - was certain our flame would regain - nope
Quickly - better find some dope - to ease that pain
Spirited revenge slide in - became my best friend
What goes around comes around - Ha! Ha! I can't wait to see this

My pathetic mistake! - Years later healing
A tough challenge - I am exhausted - Help me what's happening?
Depression - anxiety - sleepless nights - you in my sight

I'm quickly losing strength over this fight
This seems like a never-ending expensive life
How can I possibly ever be the same?

Now sadly - I am still insane - no medicine can fix this pain
The wound may heal- but this scar will remain
I am all out of faith - no luck - this sucks!

Choices - chances - changes
Too much work - I just can't forget that jerk
Every day seems to get worse! I feel numb
I must be strong- how can I become titanium?

Alas - I'll just stay safely in my cocoon
For as long as it takes-getting over these stupid mistakes
My hope is that MAYBE someday soon
I'll become that Beautiful Butterfly
As I fly off into the sunset - people will smile at me - Peacefully

EPILEPSY

It's the lack of control - the worried family running to get medication
The 2:00 a.m. phone calls because you forgot to tell them you're okay
The crippling anxiety - the severe depression - the body jerks-after a seizure
Makes you feel like your bones and muscles are wearing away

It's the fear that you won't wake up the next day
Being grateful for waking up at all-to face another day - trying to be happy
It's waking up in an ambulance- eating hospital food time and time again
It's the suffering from not being able to sleep at night

Or sometimes sleeping like a cat - just naps
It's everyone being nice to you only because
They know about your disability - don't feel sorry for me
I want to be treated like everyone else - please!

It's the girlfriend that won't leave you - the guilt she would feel
The horrid feeling when you often think - what a burden you are to her
Does she really still love me?
Is it just something that's said to ease my pain?
Yes you feel insane - damn epilepsy you're to blame!

My mind is racing - I can't stop feeling this negative B.S
This horrific drastic low self-esteem
So darn low you can't scrape yourself off the floor
The same floor you've fallen onto many times
Those severe headaches-heartaches-lost friends
How in the hell am I supposed to live like this?

EPILEPSY

Those painful thoughts inside your head that won't go away
The different personalities you become - the things you shout out to
The people you love - You don't remember what you said or why
Not ever thinking clearly before you speak
Feeling miserable inside after your outbursts-sweating
Then you just sit in the dark alone for hours and hours
Believing you must be cursed - Thinking [Do I need an exorcism?]

The feeling of weakness - mind - body and soul
Those therapists try and try - unfortunately they can't help you
It's feeling like your brain has been put in a Vitamix
It's changing medication to find the right one
Stricken terror of the unknown side effects

The neurologist is excited and willing to help
Except he just keeps giving you more and more drugs
What the heck is this the right answer? You fear not

Suddenly a woodpecker is outside - that sound is making you crazy
At times you want to walk out the door- jump off a ledge
So that you never return from all those burns
From the scars of the wounds and forgotten memories

EPILEPSY IS NOT JUST A SEIZURE
Author unknown - Some lines and comments rewritten by Lola

SOMEWHAT DARK

DO YOU SOMETIMES FEEL:

Not loved, Hopeless, Depressed, No Purpose, Fragile, Confused, Lonely, Lost, Full of Anxiety, Need to Escape, Terrified or Judged?

Or just want to sleep all the time? No appetite or overeating?

Are you sometimes annoyed when you see sweet couples together? {Stay away from the Hallmark Channel! So Predictable}

What about painful truth? That is Everywhere - Everyday!

DO YOU SOMETIMES GET UPSET WHEN PEOPLE TELL YOU TO JUST BE HAPPY AND ENJOY LIFE!!! JUST SMILE!!!

Well, this can be annoying, especially for people who don't know you very well and walk around like Mary Poppins all the time.

This becomes even more annoying for people who know you! When you didn't ask for their advice! Just makes you wonder…

Am I that awful? Then the only answer to this is to be in seclusion. That's not too weird you just don't want to bother anybody.

Be Careful! If you don't control your mind - someone else will.

YES, SOME OF US CAN NOT FEEL JOY FOR PLENTY OF REASONS!!! MANY OF US COULD FEEL RIGHT BAD NOW!!!

SOMEWHAT DARK

Dial - 988 - This is a free confidential service available to anyone in Colorado experiencing mental health issues, substance abuse, or, an emotional crisis.

Reach out for yourself or for someone you may be concerned about such as a loved one friend or neighbor.

Dial 1-844-493-8255 - Colorado Support Hotline - open 7 days a week from 7:00 a.m. until midnight - opt into the support line - to connect with a Peer Specialist.

PLEASE DO NOT DELAY THIS - YOUR FEELINGS ARE REAL

LOVE

Clara and I watched the Barbie movie together on October 27, 2023 at the Heather Gardens Clubhouse

To my dear friend Clara:

It was fate that we met and we became friends
You have proven to me what real strength is
I think of you every day and pray for you often
Your fabulous smile lights up every room
The glow that reflects from you is brighter than any candle
Therefore I don't even need a candle - because I have you near
My love for you grows stronger with each day
Thank you for everything!

With much appreciation, love, and gratitude,
Your friend forever, Lola

DEAR JUDY

This picture was taken when I visited you in San Francisco
You were my best friend from the Bronx
You never knew you were my hero
Admired you more than anyone in my life
I loved and adored you so much
My dog Sheba had pups - I gave you one
Judy named him Heineken - he was cute and obnoxious
You will always remain my loved - unique friend in so many ways
My kids called you Aunt Judy - they loved and adored you too
I miss you every day - Makes my heart ache
When I meet you at the Pearly Gates
I expect you to say - WTF?
You have no idea how hard I have fought
To keep this exact special spot

DEAR BLUE EYES

We dated for a year and a half. He's the only gentleman I ever dated
Except I was bored, young, innocent - I yearned for excitement
You were tall, handsome, and had blond hair, and blue eyes
A full-time job and working on your parents' farm - how lame
I guess that meant I wanted the bad boys - that's stupid-I found out too late

You kept your hair cut short, and you always looked amazing
All the ladies were after you, but you picked me
I wasn't even looking for a guy - I was busy with work and school.
I suppose that's what made me appealing I wasn't after you or anyone else
I was a beautiful girl - somehow I lured you in
I called you Blue Eyes - I did love you - you gave me a ring - sapphire

You were so sweet - I thought I wasn't good enough for you
Yes, I was wildly screwed up - Yet always fun to be around
I broke up with you for no reason
You continued to visit me for another year and a half
You wanted to get married and you wanted to marry me! Really? Yes

Because - I thought I wasn't worthy of you and you deserved better
I made a plan to tell you something ridiculous so you would stop seeing me
I asked you if you had tried any of the drugs going around
Like Pot - Hash - Quaaludes - Acid - Mescaline?

So I told you that I was doing them regularly -Then let out a hysterical laugh
I was having a great time with them - I said I was super high right now!
This was the most absurd lie - I could come up with was my plan
I just knew that would chase you away - forever
I couldn't believe that I looked you straight in the eyes and lied like that

DEAR BLUE EYES

As you left I never watched you walk out the door
I never heard from you again and I cried for the longest time
I knew later on in life I would regret this - I do to this day

I never met another like you a man that respected me
Treated me kindly - Would do anything for me and loved me unconditionally
Until that day I told that ridiculous lie
We could have been soulmates for life - something I have never had
I long for now and will forevermore
I guess that's because I was young and dumb!

EARTH ANGELS

A single word can open any broken heart
We all have pain - sometimes we have to forget that part
So now I look for Angels in everyday - simple search
I start my day telling myself Angels are here on earth

Maybe you can be an Earth Angel for someone else
A complete stranger someone in your path- a busy doorway
A day of many errands - starting with your favorite coffee shop
Everyone is in such a hurry-sad to see
Except this won't affect me - I'm happy to say I'm an Earth Angel in every way

Just stop just for a moment - give a glance
Find those Angels - you must give PEACE a chance
Or could you be the next Earth Angel for someone else?
Be KIND - make someone's day special - become a giver not a taker

This could be a smile from you -   give a simple compliment
To a total stranger? Oh yes yes - sometimes they could become your friend
A smile you receive or give has no price tag on it - yep it's free!
Earth Angels are everywhere - please trust me

I set out each day to make at least two people smile
They could laugh in my face - I'm silly
So what - that made me an Earth Angel again today!
You are Unique - That's what an Earth Angel told me one day
Tomorrow I know I will meet a couple of Earth Angels - along my way

EARTH ANGELS

Forever keep looking-each and everyday
Something I can count on - don't even have to pray
I Love those Earth Angels - they are always everywhere I go
Gives me a great big smile - warms my heart a glow
This heart of mine was horribly cold for the longest time
The Frigid ice almost stole my soul

That is why:
I will forever look for Earth Angels
I will forever be an Earth Angel
What if you became one too?
START TODAY!!!

Love from Lola

FIRST KISS

My very first kiss
3 months after my 13th birthday
Early morning at our nearby beach
No one was there
Just Gene and I

He was so gorgeous - adorable - charming
His dark hair complimented those green eyes
He held me ever so gently
His kiss was soft and sweet

We walked along the beach together - hand in hand
The tide was racing - loved the feel of sand on my feet
He asked me to be his girlfriend - ME?
Didn't think I was pretty enough
We graved our names together on a nearby tree
With this huge heart! WOW!

The rush was incredible - I was floating on air
We spent every day together
I went to his house - met his big family
Ate dinner with them - so cool - I Thought
Sometimes - I stayed over and shared a room with his sister

He gave me the most adorable ring - a cute flower with a pink stone
He said - Just because I love you
We always walked hand in hand at school
We were as one - everybody knew

That was the first time I ever felt important to ANYONE

FIRST KISS

I love you Gene - This is REAL - not puppy love
For Christmas - he gave me a gold necklace
I felt a rush through my whole body - We Belong Together

Everything was amazing - especially Gene and me
Finally, the school year ended - hooray - summer is finally here
Now we can spend MORE time together

Oh no - new girl moved into town - next block
Her name was Betsy that ho-ho
She was incredibly beautiful - lots more curves
He fell for her charms - ran to her arms

How could this be? I know you love me
We're still together - we didn't break up
So I walked to his house
That was a mistake - I want to know - he would explain

Instead Gene wasn't there - his mother told me
About them and said."I'm sorry."
Lost him - Lost his whole family
Wait - was this my fault? - what did I do wrong?

Stumbled home - Burned out on crying - Threw up
Humiliated - crushed - I held my cat Felica - my tears soaking her fur
Called my best friend - she said - so simple - just forget him
At times like this - best friend is not giving me the advice I need

I will never forget you - my first kiss - my first love

FIRST KISS

My broken heart - will it ever mend?
Hurried along by several chores - my single mom - works many hours
Yep - she wouldn't understand-doesn't have time-too tired

I couldn't eat - couldn't sleep-felt numb
Just thinking of how it used to be - when he only LOVED ME
How - I was finally part of a - real family

The most painful thing was - I went back to being a NOBODY
I felt dumb
FOR A VERY LONG TIME - crying - sad - can't talk to anyone
Where is the Sun? - dang - just keeps raining - I played my record again
And again - Stop in the Name of Love by The Supremes

One day - took a walk - The rain had finally stopped
Somehow - finally looked up
A rainbow - A beautiful blue jay - SINGING
She was alone - Watching her in that tree - among the wet branches

WOW! How is This little bird so strong?
Suddenly - realizing - I can be happy too - WITHOUT HIM
Thank you rainbow in the sky - thank you - Miss Blue Jay
EXCEPT - somedays - I'm still pissed off - trying to keep it on the low

                              Love-Lola

IDEAS FROM MY 3 YEAR OLD

Sometimes just sometimes - I don't know what to do with you
When I leave the room for a Split Second
She grabs a chair and climbs onto the countertops
As I walk into the room glaring - she just gives me a smile
Her big brown eyes melt me away - I say get down - she says no way

She's holding on to her favorite stuffed animal a pink unicorn
I grabbed my phone and tried to take a picture - only now she was frowning
What happened to that smile? She tells me it flew away
Like the birds outside the window - Mom
What kind of bird did you see? Her eyes open wide - A Robin!

I look outside the window - no Robin
I don't see her - I guess she flew away
My toddler tells me we need to get a bird feeder and a bird bath soon
I say but Why? Mom you're silly - so the birds can eat and take a bath
That way they'll stay longer in our yard - they won't fly away

Maybe they'll even make a nest - It's a good idea, right?
Yes - that's the best idea I've heard in a very long time
I hug her - take her off the counter - I smile
Darn it! I didn't get that photo - then as she goes off to play
I wish she would always stay - this sweet little girl

My eyes tear up - as I remember when I first walked into the room
I was not that happy with her - I was freaking furious!
Except I love my little girl and always will - no matter what
Now I realize that these little things - are the best things life can bring
She gives me such joy every day - how did she become so smart?

IDEAS FROM MY 3 YEAR OLD

We rushed off to shop the very next day-such fun and I got pics too!

MEMORIES ARE SWEET! CHERISH THEM!

To see a Robin flying can indicate a symbol of Renewal, Passion, and New Beginnings

A SINGLE MOM

I fell in love with a man - he was the love of my life
Every day was Paradise - he truly loved me - unlike anyone else
We were best friends - so I thought
He was excited - wanted to have children
We both had jobs - I knew it would be difficult to juggle
Yet I agree - because he was the love of my life
I suppose - I would do anything for him

So our family began with a little girl - YAY - we named her - Jasmine
We both kept working - We needed two incomes - she had to go to daycare
My honey said one day - I really want a son
So I got pregnant again this time a boy - YAY - we named him - Jack
We both kept working - they both had to go to daycare
I drove the kids to daycare - went to work - picked them up

I made wonderful homemade meals every night - I prepped the night before
Only - after I had helped them with their homework
Played games with them - reading books - my sweet little ones
Then I tucked them into bed - singing until they fell asleep
Then - my meal prepping - for lunches - for dinner

Excited to spend time with my honey - watching movies - making love
He was still - the love of my life and I proved it - every night
Then suddenly - my honey was not home from work yet - ever
The fear is here and it's way too near
My God I hope I'm wrong - Am I going to be a single mom?
My honey's drinking problem got worse - worse
He didn't come home from work because he was at the bar

He didn't come home from work because he was a liar

A SINGLE MOM

He didn't come home from work because he was with some whore
Even then - he was still the love of my life
I was at work one day - he came and got his clothes
He changed his phone number - his email
He unfriended me - Instagram - Facebook

He took all of OUR money out of the bank
I was devastated - except he was still the love of my life
Oh no - now I am a single mom
I did not want my kids to know - I was so SAD
So at night - after they were asleep - I cried into my pillow
Every night - I prepped the meals - for lunches- for dinner

I used all my energy - everything I had to make the best life for my kids
I took them shopping with me at the grocery store
I took them to many parks - including fantastic - water parks
We went on nature walks - zoos - magic shows - and we watched plays
Sometimes - it was difficult to see the other couples together as families

My house was - always open to their friends
I made sure - it was always SAFE
We had huge birthday parties - Halloween parties - sleepovers
I made everything from scratch - everyone raved about my cooking
I was a baker too - my cupcakes - fudge - and cookies were Heavenly
The other moms envied me because I was always cheerful

Then every night after I put the little ones to bed - I cried into my pillow
When the kids grew up - there were Proms - Homecomings
I made all the corsages and - boutonnieres too

A SINGLE MOM

I had a lot of energy - I never slowed down - I never gave up
And I still loved HIM - I thought - he'd show up

I dreamed he told me - it was all a mistake - he never forgot us
He would say - you're the love of my life - that dream never came true
Jasmine and Jack moved on to college! I'm so proud of them
They never knew their father - they were okay
And they got married - had their own little ones
I saw them - only sometimes - THEY ALL are the - loves of my life
So I cried into my pillow - every night - I do have friends but it's not the same

Family doesn't necessarily require blood it requires love!

Things got really bad for me - you see I was no longer 23
Sleeping at night became impossible for me - my doctor was able to help
Then the anxiety crept in - like a nightmare from some horror show
Those benzos kept me afloat - except you - my kids - my grandkids
Were my only hope - I cried Into my pillow every night - alone

None of you knew things were so bad for me - I didn't tell you
You were busy with your own family - work - your friends
I would get texts from you now and then - I would always respond
EXCEPT a phone call would be great - you see I grew up before
Those - darn cell phones - All of you would die - without them
I REALLY HATE TO TEXT! It's Not Personal - don't get the real message

Now I'm home alone - in my awful condo - I pray every night for all of you
I am old I don't intend to see those - Pearly Gates for quite a long time

A SINGLE MOM

Yet tomorrow is never promised - give that SOME thought
I just wish I could see all of you - I know not - all at once - you're busy
A visit now and then - would be paradise - In my eyes
Because all of you are the loves of my life!

Leaving you this letter - with tons of love from your
Single Mom and Grandma

AFRAID TO LOVE

Hello there - my name is Mandi and I'm afraid to love or be loved. I've been hurt and I don't want to go through that ever again. Except these nights have become so lonely I became hopeless. We met through a dating app. Does anyone tell the truth about those? Probably never.

After chatting for a week we decided to meet up for coffee. I suggested this little coffee house close by and we talked, he actually looked like his picture on the dating app, wow! His name was Joe he was very poised, charming and handsome.

He's got to be fake, except I was lonely, well I lied and told him I had a boyfriend who worked all the time. I was nervous so I started saying the stupidest things like "He's such a jerk, I think now the best thing to do is to break up with him." [What am I in high school again?] He told me he was single, he had been dating except had not met anyone sincere. All the women were so materialistic, and strange, with no sense of humor.
[Oh yeah I got this - I can be very funny!]

He drank his coffee black, I enjoyed mine with a bit of everything in it. He was a manager in a grocery store. [How boring] Yep - I'm boring also. I'm the manager of a clothing store. Retail is horrid, although we do have common ground there. Both of us lied about our jobs on the dating app we laughed about it. I gave him my number my actual number, not a fake one. Something was dashing about him, he was incredibly alluring, and my heart was fluttering. I made sure to laugh just a little bit.

When I got home, I couldn't get him out of my head so I got ready for bed, need sleep, busy day tomorrow. It was about 10:00 pm and he called. I was amazed he didn't just text me or not call me at all.

AFRAID TO LOVE

We spoke on the phone for an excessively long time. I told him I was tired, and he said that he wanted to meet up again and maybe have dinner did I like Italian? He said he would make a reservation for Friday night, 7:00 pm

I met him there because I didn't know him. We had a great time. this was too good to be true. We had a great dinner and wine. I told him we could go Dutch I don't expect the man to pay," No way I've got this." He glared at me with those emerald green eyes. [I desperately wanted to make love to him right there on the table] I smiled and said.

"Thank you so much this was such a lovely dinner." Joe walked me to my car, he sweetly held my hand. I wanted more, could he sense that? Before I could reach into my purse to get my keys, he pushed me up against my car and kissed me madly. OMG- This was so hot I was in flames! Then he said," Call me when you get home so I'll know that you are safe, ok?" I did that but I kept the conversation short, I didn't want to seem desperate even though I am.

We met up again a few days later, this time I asked him over for dinner that I would get takeout. I'm not sure what happened but we barely got through dinner and ended up in my bedroom. Everything happened so fast, the passion between us was beyond amazing! I felt somewhat embarrassed as he held me close after our mind-blowing sex.

Joe used my bathroom, got dressed and, kissed me goodbye. We continued this arrangement for five months, because he started to spend the night at my apartment, and sometimes I went over to his house. He had this sort of weird roommate who was hardly ever there. It was always fantastic, Joe was a great cook too. Then suddenly, I started to get some flashing red flags. Joe became demanding and talked a lot about himself, he was conceited and arrogant. So I told him I couldn't see him anymore.

AFRAID TO LOVE

He showed up on my doorstep unexpectedly one evening so we could talk. Joe gave me a beautiful bouquet of my favorite oriental lilies. He was sweet and pleaded with me. Naturally, we worked things out. We ended up between the sheets. This time our sex way was hotter than the other times before! I know he was trying to prove himself in every way.

Somehow he made me feel very suspicious. He was sneaky except I would see him texting on his phone sometimes. I thought he was seeing his ex-girlfriend and I was right, I spoke with a few ladies who saw them together at dinner, and they had photos to prove it. [Thank you cell phones] They enjoy this kind of thing, it makes them happy when other people are miserable. Except I was thankful for this.

So he was a two-timing snake! I wanted to contact her but I was afraid of him. I had to stop seeing Joe altogether. He became angry again! Why the heck is this happening to me? When I look back there seems to be a pattern here. I'm a magnet for these impossible men. I'll probably never love again. Yes, this proves that's why I'm afraid to love or be loved.

I switched jobs with a pay cut and had to start all over. Changed my phone number and moved. Exhausting! Now I was a mess and all alone again. Thanks for wrecking up my life Joe. I guess I'm bad at love. Was this his plan all along? Why am I so gullible? I want to trust people, I want to feel like the world has good people and there are, I just don't attract them.

I wanted to put him on blast all over the internet but I didn't have the strength left in me, yet I know I should have, I just needed plenty of time to heal. Except now that I'm working on taking care of myself. I'm okay with being alone. Yep, he'll find more victims, that awful covert narcissist! Be extra careful ladies they're out there. Those Doctor Jekyll and Mr Hyde personalities.

AFRAID TO LOVE

They are cruel! With no remorse. There are still no words to describe how at times, there are days when I feel like giving up! How do I stop these wrecking balls inside my brain? Not sure if I'm ready for all the work this heartache is going to take.

I don't want to go through this again. I feel like giving up. Help! Somebody, please save me! Maybe someday I'll meet my Prince Charming just because I deserve him.

YOU DON'T KNOW ME

My Darling Love:

I see you often - I'm invisible to you
Sadness - too bad you don't know me
I am kind - I'm quite amazing you'd see
A little Madness inside me - I have the stuff that you want
I am the thing that you need - begging for more

I am beautiful in my extraordinary ways
I am strong - yet gentle - funny and sincere
My laugh would make you smile
That smile would take you - many miles
I could sing you a song - you would feel like you belong

I would - listen to all your fears - wipe away your tears
Just because - I truly listen - always and forever
I'm the only one for you - then I would remind you
That you're a hero in so many ways - too bad you don't know me

I would - keep your secrets - inside my head
Just because - my heart is big and full of patience
I have a positive attitude - it shines like the sun
My glass is half full - yours is half empty
I could light up your life - if you let me in

I could warm up your soul that's so damn cold
Except you're my DARLING LOVE - inside my mind
You could never make the time - too bad you don't know me
I'm not your type - yep - you would never notice me
If you did - you would just toss me aside - just because

YOU DON'T KNOW ME

You'll never realize how much you mean to me
Always be there to hold your hand
A shoulder to cry on - If maybe you felt vulnerable
Anytime - day or night - I'm smoking HOT
Sadness - too bad you don't know me
I must get you out of my head - you are shallow
I don't need you - except yes you need me

KIKI AND KIRK

We met on a warm summer day in August. I was walking my dog, a Yellow Lab named Dolly, just taking in the sunshine. I just worked ten days in a row. Lucky for me my friendly neighbor Claudia, likes to walk Dolly. I had terrible feelings about not being around my dog, and I was riddled with guilt. So instead of enjoying this beautiful day, I was mind fogged with negative feelings, even though the sun felt so good on my skin. I was irritable and exhausted! I'm not sure what day of the week it is, maybe Sunday?

Then he came along, his dog ran up to mine and they started playing together like they've known each other forever. I was wearing some ugly raggedy clothes since I hadn't done my laundry forever nor cleaned my place. My hair was pulled back in a pink clip, and I was wearing a little bit of mascara and of course, my lip gloss, I always wear my Victoria's Secret lip gloss. The one I grabbed as I ran out the door was called Sugar High and it's sparkly. I looked hideous, and I felt like crap.

I wasn't sure that going outside and walking through the park was what I needed, I just wanted to sleep. That's what I thought until I saw HIM. He was tall, tan with deep blue eyes, and sandy blonde hair, he was wearing a green tank top, and it was very noticeable that he had been seriously working out, OMG he looks just like Ryan Gosling!

Yeah, I felt weak in the knees, with his Golden Retriever I don't know how I was standing, I started to giggle like a thirteen-year-old girl. "Hi there, wow our dogs seemed really like each other my dog's name is Dolly. What's your dog's name? Oh yeah, my name is Kiki." [Oh my gosh I sound like an idiot, I'm giggling - I'm rambling - I'm out of my mind, no I'm in shock he's so gorgeous!]

KIKI AND KIRK

I haven't dated in so long. After my last long-term boyfriend started dating one of my good friends. Everyone keeps telling me it's just a typical scenario. I told them I was not living in a reality show! So I just stopped talking to anyone except Dolly, and the coworkers that I have to accept.

[I'm certain this guy is not single]

"Hello, my name is Kirk and this is my dog Molly, nice to meet you." Then he held out his hand to shake mine. I was so sweaty and unable to speak, so I nodded politely and shook his hand. Then I started giggling again. "Oh, how cute, we have Dolly and Molly and they're becoming friends. It's adorable. [If this guy is single, I'm going to jump on him at any moment, wait a minute we're in public - oh who cares?]

"Hi, my name is Kiki, I named my dog after Dolly Parton who did you name your dog after?" The dogs continued to play together he asked me if I wanted to sit on the bench. Then he looked me straight in my eyes, I swear those big blue eyes became this deep ocean blue. I started to melt, that's when he said. "Well, I'm not sure you want to hear the reason why I named my dog Molly. I shook my head motioning yes, and became speechless.

"My dog is named Molly after the baby my wife and I had that was stillborn. It was a shock to both of us, that was four years ago. We have tried everything to have another baby. My wife became extremely unstable and turned into an alcoholic, she hasn't done much of anything and now she's divorcing me. So we're separated now."

Oh my gosh, I'm so embarrassed I just told you this I don't even know you, I'm sorry." [I almost burst into tears, this gorgeous man is heartbroken too. Well, I guess jumping him right now is not going to work, I'm so warped.]

KIKI AND KIRK

"No, no it's quite all right." I put my hand on top of his, to comfort him. Kirk looked into my eyes, as he teared up a little bit. Our dogs approached us and laid their heads on our laps spontaneously. Unbelievable.

Kirk replied, "We should get going, it's almost time for Molly's dinner."

I took out my phone and asked if it was okay if we could text later. I just knew this was my only chance, so why not, right? I quickly reached into my little backpack that carried and took out a pen and wrote my number on a pink post note, yep I like pink. That color is usually for kids or old ladies. He took out his phone and called mine.

Then he smiled at me, and I melted, what a gorgeous smile. As he walked away with Molly. I sat there frozen petting my dog, holding back my tears I told her "Let's walk a little bit and then we'll go home and have dinner."

Molly and I continued to walk, the sun was still shining, and the sky was lined with fluffy white clouds. I felt like I was floating in the air. I was so excited I started skipping along the paths. When Dolly and I got home, I fed her and gave her some treats, my stomach had butterflies. I wanted to text him right away but I knew it was too soon, yes I'll wait a couple of hours. I was anxious and excited. Then I sobbed, wow, I needed to do that. I wanted to call a friend to tell them about Kirk but I didn't have any, none I could trust. Yeah, I have incredible trust issues, along with some other issues that I hide extremely well, but doesn't everybody? Maybe.

At 7:30 Kirk texted me - Would you like to come over for dinner Saturday night? If you're free, please bring Dolly. Do you like salmon? I waited 5 minutes to respond as my heart was pounding. I replied just a minute let me check my calendar, yeah okay Saturday will work.

KIKI AND KIRK

Yes, love salmon. I immediately ran to my closet to figure out what to wear. I'm a pescatarian and I did not tell him that, this man is just amazing! Then, Saturday evening finally arrived and I put on a nice black dress, fixed my hair, and put on makeup, I looked and felt remarkable. I walked in with a fabulous bottle of chilled white wine. His house was fantastic and extremely clean. [Did he even live here?]

Kirk opened the door with a smile and said. "You look so beautiful thank you for joining me this evening." The table was set with a freshly sliced baguette, Irish butter, and plenty of lemons. Everything was so perfect I got the jitters, quite frankly, this flawless environment made me sort of nervous, but I'm not sure why. Then I gave him the bottle of wine. He proceeded to open the cupboard and get out a new box of wine glasses. [oh my gosh he doesn't drink]

Kirk opened the wine and poured a little bit for himself, and a smidgen more for me. We sat on the couch, and he said "I like you Kiki, I know we just met, I love to cook and I hope we can take this slowly, I haven't dated anyone. This divorce is exhausting and my job is very demanding." [Seriously? he was deeply sincere, okay I'm going to put my trust issues aside and enjoy this time with him]

I felt my eyes becoming dilated, here I was sitting on the couch with this incredible man, ready to have dinner and I didn't know what to say. So I asked," What kind of work do you do?" He told me he was an aerospace engineer. [At that time I started to wonder, now he's brilliant too?] I wanted to leave because I'm a cashier at Home Depot, I write and illustrate children's books. I am quite skillful at this, probably because I'm so childlike at times. I've made some decent money from this which is nothing compared to his job, except when I told him, he said it was phenomenal that I was an author and an artist.

KIKI AND KIRK

We had a lovely dinner, both the dogs played, and then we cleaned up the dishes together, I had more wine he didn't. I said, "This dinner was delicious." Kirk told me that he could drive me home if I felt tipsy. I told him I was fine, so he walked me to my car gave me a couple of yellow roses, and kissed me on the cheek. [Again I wanted to jump him but I didn't, this man has a lot of healing to do.] he asked if we could meet at the park the next day with the dogs at about 2:00 p.m., I was thrilled and uttered, "Of course."

I couldn't wait until the next day to see him, I was going out of my mind all night just thinking about Kirk. He wanted to take it slow I wanted to take it fast. We continued meeting at the park on Sundays with the dogs, he was very chilled for a man who's going through so much. We held hands walking around, that was IT for many weeks. We started just talking about simple things like the nice weather and my books, he wanted to see them and the artwork I had done.

Kirk was so kind and nice, it was scary and I don't know why, [oh yeah I have trust issues.] Sometimes I drive by his house to see if another car is in the driveway, yep, and that's called stalking. No cars. No cars. I can't believe I'm doing this!

Okay, the walks in the park are great and the dogs are fun but it is going far too slow - for me anyhow. So I needed a plan. The next time we met at the park I told him "Do you want to see my artwork? "We can have dinner at my place on Saturday." he agreed and seemed excited.

Now I'm not the greatest cook so I got takeout from an exquisite Italian restaurant and spent a ton of money on it, of course, it was going to be worth it. I really like this man so far. I could hardly wait, and I worked on a new painting, a beach scene something I started a long time ago yeah I had no reason to finish it but now I do!

KIKI AND KIRK

Kirk arrived promptly at 7:00 p.m., We had a fabulous dinner I mentioned to him that I got carry out. I was spending my time working on a project. He told me that was just fine. "So what's the project you've been working on.?" "I bragged "Look over to your right," My painting was superb, probably the best I've ever done in life. "When he looked at it his jaw dropped. "Kiki that is incredible, wow! I love it." I moved in and planted one on him. Giggling then muttered, "Thank you, I was thinking of you the whole time I was painting it, you know like we were on the beach together." There are no beaches we live in Colorado but we love it here! This time I didn't have any wine, even though red wine would have been great. We cleaned up the dishes together, he was just so nice, that I had to figure out my next move. I showed him another painting, I had done in my art room, Kirk was definitely impressed. Then I led him by his hand to my bedroom to show him more paintings.

Kirk looked around my room and was astounded. I had sexy music playing on the Alexa, then I seduced him. [Yes that was my plan] It's a good thing I had my ceiling fan on because it got damn hot in here. We made love twice, our bodies were everywhere. We cuddled for an hour afterward. We were laughing, sharing about how extraordinary we felt, and started talking about our dogs again. He also loved the paintings on my walls. Yeah, they're pretty good, none for sale. Then he told me that he was sorry that he had to leave soon, to get Molly home. The dogs had quietly fallen asleep together in my living room. Kirk kissed me goodbye, this time not on the cheek ha-ha. He also told me he couldn't wait to see me again and would call me before going to sleep. We talked for about an hour.

I was on cloud nine I wasn't sure my plan would work, except it did. I couldn't wait for his divorce to be final. This FINALLY happened a month later. I didn't ask him any questions about it I just wanted to see him more and more.
I figured he was paying spousal support so it's none of my business.

KIKI AND KIRK

Women like to talk about everything and men don't like to talk about their finances above all things. We went to a few plays, art galleries, and museums and took Ballroom dancing classes together, which was fun. Now we go out dancing together too. Then we ventured out and took some hikes with our dogs, they did great. [Oh I forgot to mention I started working out a lot from the first day I saw him, painful but worth it]

We've been dating for almost a year now. I found a better job working at the front desk in a nearby hospital, with regular hours and no overtime, plus much better pay. Kirk does have to work some extra hours but he always makes time for me. He is sweet, kind, gentle, a great cook, and a passionate yet playful lover. I found the man of my dreams when I wasn't even looking. I think possibly our dogs brought us together.

Anyway, we fell madly in love. Except we don't live together we both agreed on this. We are currently looking into a vacation to the Key West Dog Beach. I'm living a fairy tale, I found my knight in shining armor when I wasn't even looking. You just never know.

BUTTERFLY

I am one beautiful butterfly, when you see me your eyes open wide, you stop for a moment and forget about everything.

I make you happy, even if it's just for a short time. As I flutter by up into the sky over to the next flower.

I pick up pollen from my legs and transfer it to the next flower aiding in the pollination process.

Grateful to give you a moment of smiles!
Reminder from a Butterfly - Look For The Sweetness In Life!

Made in United States
Troutdale, OR
03/16/2024

18516837R00058